# Nubia

## real one

Written by
L.L. McKinney

Illustrated by
Robyn Smith

Cover Color by
Bex Glendining

Interior Color by
Brie Henderson
with Robyn Smith
and Bex Glendining

Lettered by
Ariana Maher

**Sara Miller** Editor
**Steve Cook** Design Director - Books
**Megen Bellersen & Monique Narboneta** Publication Design

**Marie Javins** Editor-in-Chief, DC Comics
**Michele R. Wells** VP & Executive Editor, Young Reader

**Daniel Cherry III** Senior VP - General Manager
**Jim Lee** Publisher & Chief Creative Officer
**Don Falletti** VP - Manufacturing Operations & Workflow Management
**Lawrence Ganem** VP - Talent Services
**Alison Gill** Senior VP - Manufacturing & Operations
**Nick J. Napolitano** VP - Manufacturing Administration & Design
**Nancy Spears** VP - Revenue

**NUBIA: REAL ONE**

**Content notes:** The following story includes depictions of racial injustice, sexual harassment, police brutality, and an active school shooter. To anyone impacted by these issues, we encourage you to use our list of resources at the end of the book for support.

DC Comics, 2900 West Alameda Ave., Burbank, CA 91505
Printed by LSC Communications, Crawfordsville, IN, USA. 1/15/21.
First Printing.
ISBN: 978-1-4012-9640-7

Library of Congress Cataloging-in-Publication Data

Names: McKinney, L. L. (Leatrice L.), writer. | Smith, Robyn (Cartoonist), illustrator. Glendining, Bex, colourist. | Henderson, Brie, colourist. | Maher, Ariana, letterer.
Title: Nubia : real one / written by L.L. McKinney ; illustrated by Robyn Smith ; cover color by Bex Glendining ; interior color by Brie Henderson; lettered by Ariana Maher.
Description: Burbank, CA : DC Comics, [2021] | Audience: Ages 13-17 | Audience: Grades 10-12 | Summary: Nubia has always stood out because of her Amazonian strength, but even though she uses her ability for good she is seen as a threat, so when her best friend Quisha is threatened by a boy who thinks he owns the town, Nubia risks everything to become the hero society tells her she is not.
Identifiers: LCCN 2020040023 | ISBN 9781401296407 (trade paperback)
Subjects: LCSH: Graphic novels. | CYAC: Graphic novels. | Ability--Fiction. | Identity--Fiction.
Classification: LCC PZ7.7.M44226 Nu 2021 | DDC 741.5/973--dc23

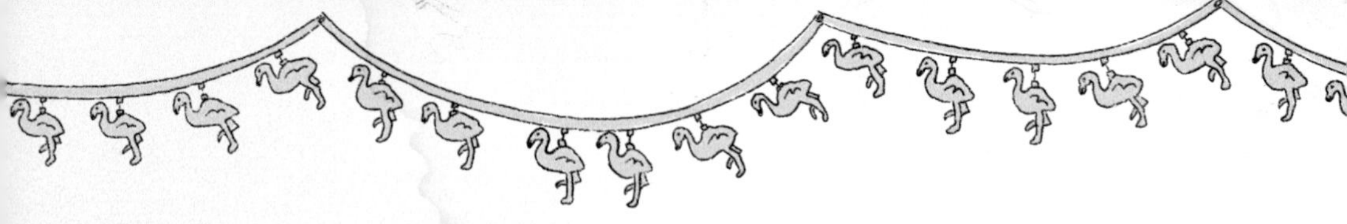

## It's time for Nubia, for a *real one*.

I never thought I could be a superhero. I never thought I could save the cat, my neighborhood...or the world. I never thought people who looked like me got chances to do *those* things. Growing up a Black American girl in the Maryland suburbs, I was the fly in the milk, looking for grand adventures outside my bedroom window.

The pages of books held the only mischief and magic my mother allowed in the house. But every weekend, my nerdy father took me to the bookstore and comics shop where I filled up on sorcery, dragons, extraterrestrial beings, alternate futures... and superheroes. I collected all the cards, kept the precious, glossy comics in their clear sleeves (just like my dad!), and made sure they were *always* in the proper order.

I was happy to live within these colorful pages, a place far more entertaining than my quiet childhood. I was desperate to be part of it all.

But I couldn't find myself...until Nubia.

My dad handed me a Wonder Woman comic and flipped open to a special spread. I'll never forget the way my little-girl heart backflipped at the sight of her—Nubia. Beautiful and Black like me. Like my mother. Like my grandmothers. Like my aunties. I fell in love.

That single image told me that I, too, could save the world.

L.L. McKinney's *Nubia: Real One* is the story I needed as a teen *and* the one I need now. Witty, powerful, and revolutionary, this book reminds us that not everyone gets an invitation to be a hero, but everyone deserves to be one. Seeing artist Robyn Smith's rendering of young Nubia made my heart do that backflip again. I was a little girl once more.

This book is a tinderbox ready to ignite a heroic flame in every heart. A reminder that there's a cape and costume awaiting us all.

It's time for Nubia, for a *real one*. So that we may be like her. The world needs us!

**The world needs you!**

Dhonielle Clayton

*New York Times* bestselling author of the Belles series and
COO of the nonprofit organization We Need Diverse Books

For everyone who has loved Nubia since the beginning and to all the new fans falling for her now, we outchea.

**—L.L. McKinney**

To my cousin, Toni, the inspiration for Nubia's character design, my parents, my brother, my family and friends. Thanks for the constant support and giving in to all my reference picture demands.

**—Robyn Smith**

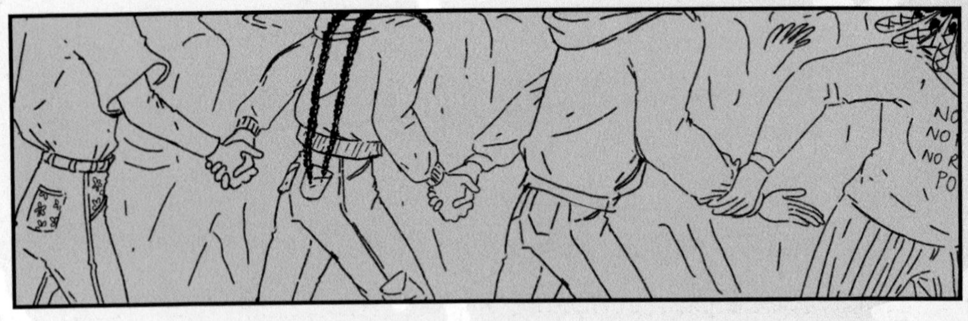

# PART I

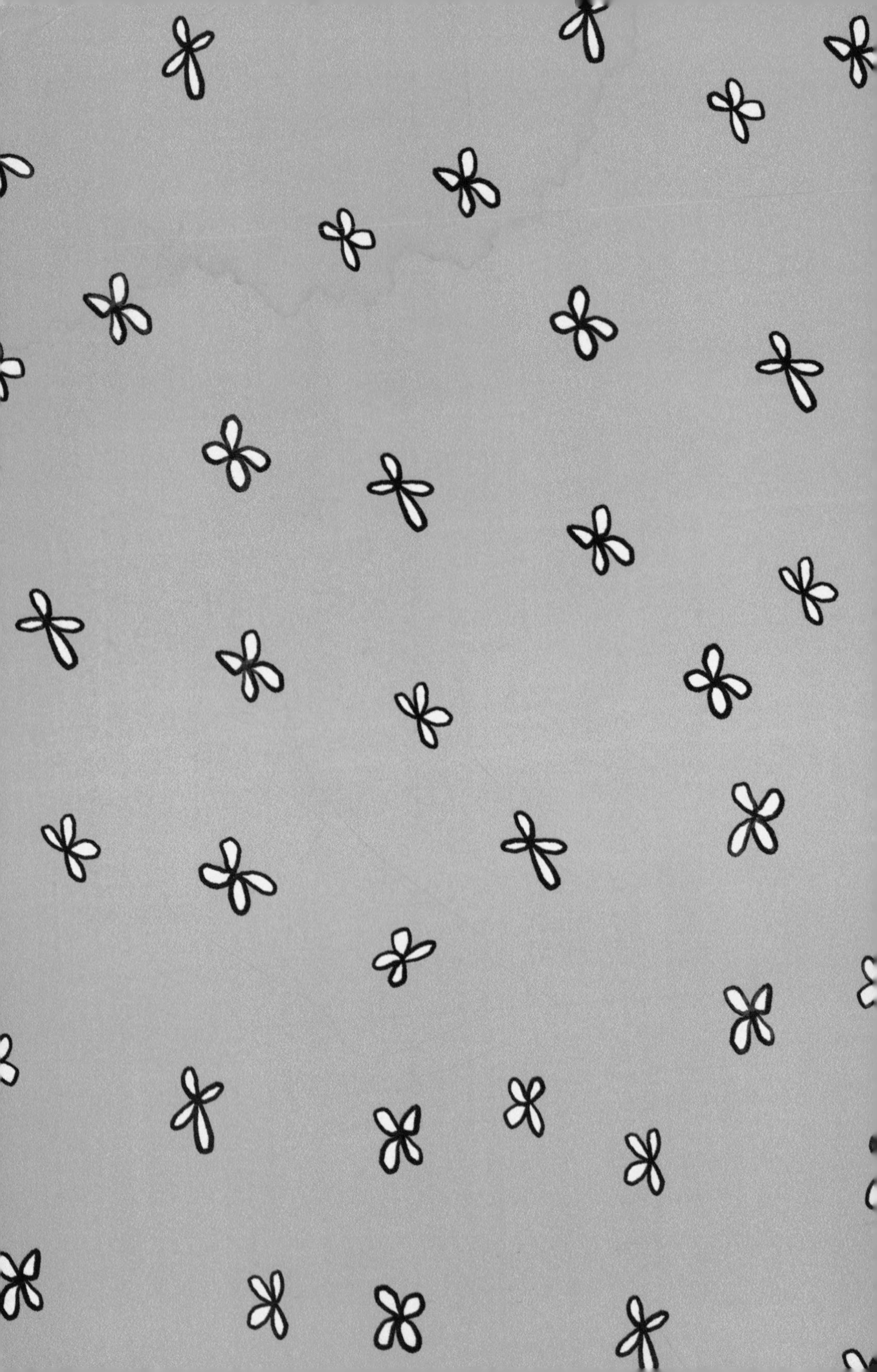

Nubia, you tellin' me you actually ***wanna*** work all summer?

I'm tellin' you I wouldn't mind, but my moms would.

Here we go.

Mama Amera already talkin' 'bout it's best if I find something safe and quiet to do with my time.

Sooooo, something boring.

Exactly!

You got any ideas what you wanna do?

Not really. But whatever it is, they'll kill my whole vibe.

Oooooooh, Nikeeeee!
Lissen, it took me forever to get in, and if I flake Pops'll beat me to death with his wallet for wasting his money like that.
So I feel for Nubia, but my hands are tied.

It's cool. I just don't wanna be stuck at home like I'm under house arrest. I even suggested a family vacation, but noooooooo.
You're free to come with me and my sisters.
Driving cross-country crammed into a tinkertoy? No offense, but that actually sounds worse than hypothetical house arrest.

It'll be *fun!* Do some sightseeing, some hiking, some protesting.
One of these things is not like the other.
TIZZLERS

Protesting is good for you. Good for the soul.
'Til tear gas canisters and rubber bullets start flying.
He's got a point.

No one said it'd be easy, just necessary.
And these "grown-ass" grown-ups ain't doing nothing, so it's on us.
Yaaaaaaasss.
SNAP
SNAP
SNAP

Is this you saying you'll come?
I would, but y'all know my moms. I'm not going nowhere without at least one of them along for the ride.
And *they* know you're seventeen, right? Only one year before you can die for your country.
And four before you can drink! Legally.
Speaking of drink, you gonna finish that?
They know. They just worried.
And for good reason.
Well, if Atlanta's too far, least y'all can do is be active in your own backyard.
Meaning?
There's a march this weekend.
Matter of fact, I'm helping put it together. So be a good friend and show up!
I'm trying to not be a dead daughter!
Wait...

This 'cause of what happened last Friday?
Yeah...

*Which* thing that happened last Friday?
That shooting over off tenth?

"A boy who had nothing to do with it was cornered and questioned by police. He got scared and ran."

"They shot him in the back."
"Right, right... Quentin. I knew him from when I stayed with my grandmom."

He was a kid. And they stay killing kids, so kids should be marching.
Yeah. It's mostly people from the area, his family, friends, people from school.
I hear you. You said this weekend?
My moms already said I couldn't go. I'll try asking again, but...

It's okay. I get it. And speaking of your grandma, Jason, I promised I would come get some sweet potato pie this weekend.
You mean *my* sweet potato pie?
Not my piece.
They all my pieces.
These two are an absolute mess, but they're *my* mess. It's like we've been running since diapers, even if it's only been a few years.
You need to learn to share!
No means *no*, LaQuisha!
bzz
bzz
They've known each other forever, though, which is why Jason gets that faraway, lovesick look when Quisha goes all activist.
He thinks I don't notice, but I do.
It's kinda cute but kinda sad.
Ugh...
What?
Wayland, with his tiresome ass.
And why haven't you blocked him, again?
I did. He just made another account to message me from. Ignoring him only makes him try harder.
You want me and the boys to make sure he gets the point?
No, it's cool, I can handle myself. Thanks, though.
*Nubia!*
YUMMY GUMMY

Hey.
H-hey. Hi, Oscar.
'Sup, Jason, hey, Quisha.
S'good?
Heeeeeeey.
...
What?!
You look like you could use a refill.
I don't—
Jason! We gotta go.
What?
We got that project we're supposed to start on, remember?
What proje—
Oomph!
The. Project. Remember.
Ow...
So why don't you go in there and get. Your. Slurp. On. If you know what I mean.
That's not—!

Text me soon as you leave.
This is oppression.

I love you, bai!
Woman, if you don't sit down and buckle up—

ZOOOOOOM

This is fine. It's just a refill.

Nothing scary about a refill. Not like he'll think I'm being weird and creepy, it's just a refill.

Calm down. It's fine.

They left. They really left! Guess I'm supposed to walk home?

I like walking! And my house is close, so...
Yeah.

BING BONG

Stop talking to yourself, weirdo.

Okay, what do I say? Hi?
No, said that already.
What's your favorite candy! Really? Fancy meeting you here!
Okay, now this is just pathetic.
FREE REFILLS
Ahem.
Sorry! Grabbing a refill.
taptaptaptap
This is ridiculous. Why am I doing this? I should go.
Yeah. Just pretend this didn't happen. Before he sees—
Everybody get on the ground!
—me.

Hands up, ***now!***

Everyone cooperates, everyone makes it out alive.

You go near that phone, I put a bullet through your eye, okay?

The rest of you get over here, and get on the ground. Don't look at me, don't look at him, look at the floor.

Ow! Hey, easy, man!

Oh, I'm sorry. Let me help you shut up.
Oscar! No...

I said keep your head down. It doesn't look down.
Hnnng!

Do something, Nubia...Come on!
Do someth—

How 'bout I blow your—
Hey, asshole.

Hold this for me.

BAM

Hurk!!
CRASH

Hey! What's going on out there?!
ONLY
jiggle jiggle

My money!
Thief!
Thief!
Wait, what?
CLICK
EHN EHN EHN
No. No no no no!

Dang kids!
Sorry!

Damn it, Nubia.
***How*** could you be so stupid? What if there were cameras in that store?
And Oscar... he saw you.
Someone ***saw*** you.
Just like last time...

GNN
WW saves the DAY
Granted, you **chose** to expose yourself. All for a pretty face...
Superheroes are pretty dope, huh?
The dopest. Super-strength, super-speed, flying?

Have you ever...met one?
No. But if I did, I'd probably lose it.

Who's your favorite?
Wonder Woman, no contest.
Why?

Strong **and** beautiful? I'd let her lay me out anytime.
And you wouldn't be upset or nothing?
Nope! I'd be honored or some junk.

Let's...go outside. I wanna show you something.

It's like I haven't learned nothing.
Like I don't know better.
Can't just leave well enough alone.

Maybe they would've taken the money and left!
It would've been fine!
Then I could've gotten outta there, but I had to go chucking A.T.M.s at folk. Mama Amera's gonna kill me...
WHOOP-WHOOOOOOP!
Nononono, NO!

Let me see your hands.
CE

Did you hear or see anything about a robbery happening at a convenience store nearby?
Uhm...

Put your arms down, slow.
Keep your hands where I can see 'em.

So you weren't anywhere near the E.Z. Shoppe over on the other side of Brenson?
Kids like us get shot. Kids like us get shot.

The clerk gave a description of one of the thieves.
...
And it matches you pretty closely.
POLICE

*Sigh*
She even described your shirt.
Kids... like us... get shot.
See, you crying like this makes me think you've got something to hide, and you don't want me finding out.
K-kids... shot...

Okay. Get up. Arms behind your back.
Since you're being so helpful, you can stay with me while I sort this out.
click click click

POLICE

Don't try anything. I'm watching you. Heh.
CE

KAZZAT
I've got a potential suspect in custody, African American female, uncooperative, stand by.
KAZZAT
POLICE

This can't be happening.
This *can't* be happening.
Damn it, Nubia.

Okay, slow down. Stop.
Breathe. Like Mama Danielle showed you.

You didn't do anything.

You. Didn't. Do anything.

But you're still in the back of the cop car.
Bet that lady wouldn't call the cops on Superman...

She took one look at me and that was it.
I was doing so good up 'til now...

CLICK!

According to witnesses, two men were responsible for the robbery.
Seems the clerk mistook one of the hostages for their accomplice.

One witness in particular was adamant you weren't part of it.
Oscar...

You're lucky, you understand?
Y-yes, sir.

Guess you're free to go.
This time. Stay out of trouble.
Just... go?
LICE

Soup's on.

Oooohhh, it smells so good in here.
Moussaka! Trying a new recipe.
Does Nubia know you're making moussaka?
I didn't say anything. She should be home soon, though, it's a school nigh—

SLAM

Did you smell it or something? Breaking down the door like that.
If I have to replace more hinges, you're paying for them.
Mer...
Mer.
Because I know you know better, even when you're hungry, and—
Amera!
Nubia, baby, what's wrong?
Sniffle
Sniffle

I-I...
I just...
I w-wanted to h-help...

I'll get you some water. You need to stay hydrated.
Deep breaths, baby. Deep breaths. Come sit down.

Now, tell us what's going on.
I-I...I messed up.
What do you mean?

There was an incident. At the E.Z. Shoppe.
You said you weren't hurt!
I'm not!
What kind of *incident?*

A...robbery. I tried to stop it.
Oh my.
Nubia.
We talked about this.

But that wasn't the problem.
Oh, okay, well, great. In that case, do I want to know what *was?*
Mer...

I didn't want to tell them. I knew what would happen if I did. How we'd have to pack up and disappear in the middle of the night because I got caught again. Leave my friends, leave our lives.
I didn't wanna tell...
But fear shook the words loose, and they poured outta me.
He *handcuffed* you?!
While he talked to officers on the scene. Some witnesses said there wasn't no girl robber, and he let me go.
I don't give a damn, it's illegal to question a minor alone!
First things first, let me start by saying I'm happy you're safe and unharmed.
Uh-oh...
Now let me ask, just how did you *stop* the robbers? You left that part out.
I...maybe... threw an A.T.M. at one of them?
... *Ahem* All right. Damage control.

Did the cop ask your name or where you lived?
No.
Did he ask for your birthday or any other personal information?
No.
Mer...
Don't "Mer" me about this, Danielle. We both know how these things work.
But it was—
We have rules for "incidents" like this for a reason.
Don't get involved. Leave the area immediately.
I know, I know.
And rule number *one.* What's rule number one, Nubia?
Avoid any and all situations that might expose me or my powers.
Throwing A.T.M.s definitely counts as something that might expose you!
They were going to *hurt* people. I...I couldn't let them. I'm sorry.
No one is upset with you, baby.
Right, *Amera?*
*sigh*
No, no. I'm not upset with you, Nubia, I'm just... upset.

I'm upset that this happened at all.
You didn't do anything wrong.
But we all know doing the right thing while looking the wrong way is enough.
We can't afford to take these chances. You can't afford to take them.
I-I'm sorry. I'm so sorry.
Stop apologizing. We're just happy you're all right.
Did anyone see you?
Oscar...
No. Everyone was on the ground.
You said the clerk blamed you.
She saw me *after* I threw the A.T.M. Money went everywhere—I think that's why she thought I was a thief.
I'll call D, see if there were any cameras we need to worry about. Or, gods forbid, any phones...
Did you eat? Mer made moussaka. You should eat.
Mama Amera must be *real* worried if she's calling D.
The two of them work together for Prince Technologies on some "If I told you, I'd have to kill you" type stuff. Whenever videos or something needs disappearing, they call D. Then they call U-Haul.
I really hope that doesn't happen this time...

Besides my parents, D is the one constant in my life. And has more of a say than I ever get, which is some mess.
He handcuffed my baby, D, of *course* I want something done. Fine. I'll meet you there.

And where are you going?
Gonna make sure our girl's in the clear.
This can't wait until after dinner?

Not if we want to stay ahead of things.

I'm sorry for messing up.
But the clerk. And the cop!
We told you, this wasn't your fault.
Why can't I mind my own business?

Nubia Johnson. You have a good, strong heart, and you care about people. That's nothing to be ashamed of.
Even if it keeps getting me into trouble?
How do you mean?
I was hidden. I could've just let the robbers take the money and go.
Why didn't you?

They were hurting...
People...They were hurting people.
And you think you could've just let that happen?
Obviously not... But maybe I should from now on. Especially if I help people and they call the cops on me.
There are other ways to help, you know.
Like that protest you mentioned, the one happening this weekend?

I think you should be able to support your friends, if you want to.
Wait, *for real?*
Thank you!
So long as you don't draw attention to yourself. I'll talk to Mer about it.
Thankyou thankyouthank you!
All right! All right, settle down.

But in all seriousness.
You're special, Nubia. And not just because of your powers, but because of who you are. Because of who came before you.
Black women have always been looking out for others. Sometimes it's a thankless, tiresome, dangerous task, but here we are.
My mother used to say, "Life started in Africa, so Black women are protective of it."
That is a gift, not a curse, and you, ***Nubia,*** are truly gifted.
LASOX

You think these "gifts" are why I keep risking my neck for total strangers? Not just me screwing up?

You are ***not*** a screw up, you hear me?
Y-yeah, I do, I just—I don't know what I'm supposed to ***do.*** We got the rules, but that's not...
Not what?

Not...***enough.*** I know you and Mama Amera are trying, really, but I think this would be easier if I could talk to someone more...like me.

Like Supergirl or Wonder Woman.
But they're probably off doing things like plugging volcanoes and preventing alien invasions, or whatever.

Do you remember the story of how we first found out you were special?
You mean with the neighbor's cat?

You were maybe three, and you loved that critter, more than they did, I'm sure.
So, one day, poor thing gets stuck up a tree, just a-yowling. And you were so distraught.
I honestly don't remember this.
WONDER WRAP

Oh, I do.
Especially the part where you pushed that tree clean over.
Haha!
Tore the dang thing up from the roots!
The look on their faces, the look on Mer's face! Priceless.
There are amazing people in the world with amazing abilities. Imagine our surprise to find out this little bitty thing that came into our lives was one.
That's when we knew we were truly blessed.

The world's not fair, and there's nothing I can do about that, but I promise you this—
No matter what's going on out there, you're free to be yourself within these walls.

Super-strength, super-speed, and a super heart. You're perfect just the way you are.
I love you, Mom.
I love you too, baby.

Nubiaaaa, my widdle Nubia. My itty-witty widdle Nubnubs!
Maaaaaaaaaa!! Really, right now?

What? I'm your mom. You can be yourself *and* my little Nubs!
Now go on, do some TikTok or whatever y'all do to relax.

BRRRRRRRING
I feel a way that you didn't text me last night.
Then you just walked past me—
Us.
*Us*...with barely a word in homeroom this morning.
Did something happen with Oscar?

What? Wh-what do you mean?
Did he come at you sideways or something?
Because he can get his with the rest of these chumps.

No, it's cool.
I mean, it's ***not,*** but I can't very well say that, now can I?
Then what's got you all long-faced? You ain't even touched your pizza, and you ***love*** that nasty mess. Almost as much as Jason.

I...didn't get to talk to him. I went inside but chickened out at the last minute.
Kinda lucky you did. Heard the place was robbed.

What in the—you didn't get caught up in that, did you? Are you okay?!
I'm fine. It must've happened after I left.
I wonder if Oscar saw anything.
I sure as hell hope not.

Did y'all...hear any details about what happened?
TRAYS HERE ↓↓↓
Just a couple white boys in masks who got their shit *wreck'd.*
That's it? Nothing else?
One of them needed an ambulance. Got arrested at the hospital.
People already making memes.
Honestly, with superheroes running around, you gotta be three kinds of stupid to try something like that in broad daylight.
That's what I was telling my—
Okay, Oscar saw me. I *know* he saw me. And I know he knows I know he saw me. But...

Nubia.
He just ain't told nobody? I guess if he did, it'd be all over the school by now.
So what's he waiting for?
Nubia...
Oh shit, what if he wants to blackmail me? On some real *Scandal*-type stuff?!
Nubia!

Damn, girl, you get lost in there?
Uh, yeah. Sorry, you say something?
I said you should check on Oscar, see if he's okay.

Oh...
I mean, that's just what a good friend would do.
If nothing else, it's what a potential blackmail victim would do.
Yeah, I guess. Aight, I'll check on him.
Now, on to some official business. I need a little help getting things together for the protest.
What kinda help?
Making signs, that sort of thing.

Would be nice if whoever had time to save corner stores could be bothered with saving actual people, like Quentin.
I wasn't there that night. And even if I was, if I tried something? Well...
They'd be marching for both of us this weekend.
Quentin ran because he was afraid.
I know what that feels like.
And now being scared while Black is a death sentence...

CLANG
211
I'm normally not into house parties, but it's s'posed to be at some rich girl's place out south.
213
So, you're counting on some free food, then?
Mmmmmmaybe. Also general good times to be had.
I guess it sounds like fun. Some chill time before the protest.
Exactly! Plus, I always been curious what them big houses look like on the inside.
What about you?
What about me?
You know Nubia ain't 'bout that party life.
Says who?!
Says the fact that you never go, no matter how many times we ask.
I mean... she's not wrong.
*If* you go to one party this year, it's gotta be this one. Especially since you're gonna be on house arrest all summer.
Maybe...
Plus, I have it on good authority that Oscar will be there.
O-oh?

And what authority is that?
The Jason-needs-to-shut-up-and-mind-his-business authority.
Not familiar with that one.
I'll give you something to get familiar with.
It's cool if you can't hang, though. I know how your moms be.
South Side parties *do* tend to end up with a million videos everywhere.
Yeah, but... Oscar will be theeeere.
On the other hand...
I never do parties. One would be...nice?
Okay, okay, I'll think about it.
Just think about it?
That's what I said, Quisha.
That's what she said, *Quisha.*
Boy, if you don't—
I gotta get across the building for Chem. See y'all later.
You two are honestly adorable together.
Two? What two, there's no two. And there's no together.
Mmmmhmmm. If you say so. Still cute, though.
Shut up. We're gonna be late.

Not fun being on the receiving end, is it, matchmaker?
Lissen, you the one that needs help—
Quisha!

Speaking of needing help... escape to the restroom?
He'd probably just wait for us.
Well, that's not creepy.

Hey, you didn't text me back.
I was busy— do you need something?
I need you to go with me to Tammy's party this weekend.
Wayland, we talked about this.

I know, I know, figured I'd shoot my shot anyway.
You been shooting all year.

Been missing, too.

Nothing wrong with a man seeing what he wants and going after it.
Quisha's a who, not an it.
Who're you, again?
You know Nubia. And I can't go with you to the party, cause I promised to go with her.
Say what now?
Yeah. Remember, you asked me to go and I said yes.
Uhhh...
So, I already have a date. Sorry, Wayland, maybe I'll see you there.
Uh-huh...Playing hard to get? Cute. Real cute.
*Why* don't you tell that Neanderthal to go screw himself? Or at least to leave you alone.
He's not worth it.
Not worth what? He called you an it! Acted like you were something he could just snatch off a shelf.
I don't wanna end up like Maria...

You think he did it?
You think he didn't?
I think Maria didn't break her arm doing no basic cartwheel. She's a whole Olympic gymnast.
I just don't get why she's protecting him by lying about it being an accident.
What do you mean?
Not anymore.
She's probably protecting herself.
He probably promised to do worse if she said anything. With his family's money and connections, that's no empty threat.
So, what, you just put up with him forever?
Only until he graduates in a few weeks. It could be worse.
I don't wanna talk about Wayland anymore.
Let's talk about what you're wearing to this party.
I never said—
You gotta go so Wayland won't know I lied!
Nnnnnnnnfiiiiiiiine. I'll ask if I can go.
Ayyyyy! You're in for a treat. I happen to be a fabulous date.
If fabulous is another word for a lot.

Okay. You can do this. You can totally do this.
It's just a party. One silly little, not that deep, party.

Just ask. No harm in asking.
The worst they can say is no. Ugh, what if they say no?!

Background check on the clerk shows she lives in *this* neighborhood. Just one block over.

She might not even recognize Nubia from the store. It could just...go away.
Maybe. D said if this grows into an issue it might be best for us to move.
Mer, it's her junior year. Nubia's flourishing, she has friends, she studies hard, she has the closest thing to a normal life for someone like her!

I know. Which is why I don't want to do that. I don't want to put you through that, put *her* through that. Not again.

I'll handle it. I...I don't know how just yet but I'll— maybe D and I can figure something else out.
If anyone can, it's my Mer.

KNOCK
KNOCK
KNOCK

Can I come in?
Of course.

Hope I'm not interrupting.
Sure you do.

What is it, baby?
I need to ask you guys something. Nothing bad! Just...

There's a party this weekend. It's *the* party, last one of the year.
Since Jason and Quisha are leaving this summer, and I'm gonna be stuck in the house, I reeeeeeally wanna go.
Kick it with my friends, de-stress after yesterday. You know, self-care.
Please?

Absolutely not.
What?!
The *last* thing you need is to be in a crowded place, likely unsupervised, beset by adolescent hormones, poor impulse control, and shenanigans.
It's just a party!

It's never just a party, or just *anything,* and you know that.
The best thing to do right now is lay low, hope everything blows over. Prepare for the worst, should it happen.

B-but...Mama Danielle...?
Your mother's right, baby. It's too risky.
All those kids means a lot of phones, and that's a lot of chances someone could catch you doing something.

Like what, dancing? Laughing? Heaven forbid I get caught having a good time!
Watch it...

I just wanna have fun with my friends. What's the problem?
No problem, until one of those friends secretly records you lifting a Buick over your head...

Th-that's not fair.

I thought you were lying when you said you had powers.
Well... I wasn't.
Dang, li'l ma. What else can you do?
Mark!

CRASH
Oh my god! You threw a car at my son!

Mom! It wasn't even like that!
You tried to crush my baby, you *freak!*
I...I wasn't g-gonna hurt—

Why am I being punished for simply *existing?!*
Nubia, it's not—
You say stuff like: Nubia, be yourself. Nubia, live your life. Then you keep me locked up like I'm the problem! Just lie to my *FACE! You can't—*

Wait a—*just who do you think you're talking to?*
...
That's what I thought. We said *no* party. End of discussion.
And since you think you can raise your voice in this house, you can't leave your room for a week.

School, bedroom. Bedroom, school. Am I understood?
Yes, ma'am.
Good. Go on, before you catch more than a case.
Y-yes, ma'am.

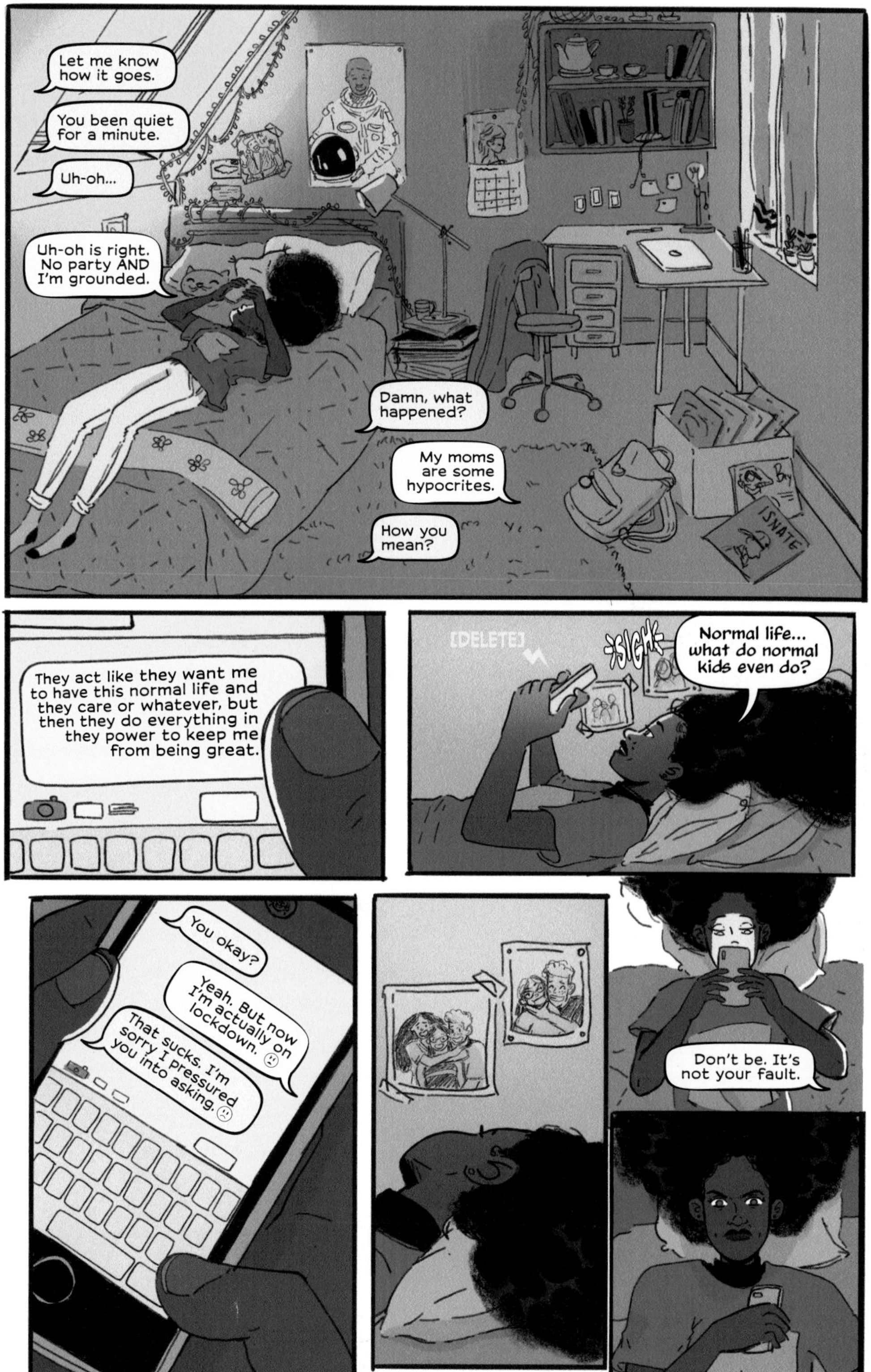

Let me know how it goes.
You been quiet for a minute.
Uh-oh...
Uh-oh is right. No party AND I'm grounded.
Damn, what happened?
My moms are some hypocrites.
How you mean?

Besides, it'll suck worse if I get caught, so you and Jason need to help me sneak out.
Wayment.
You wanna sneak out?
YOU wanna sneak out?

That so hard to believe?
Have you met you?
Shut up.

Shut up.
Wow. Rule-obeying, law-abiding Nubia wanna buck the system. This is... I need a minute.
You gonna help or naw?
Leggo.

# PART II

Friday!
Whew, you made it.
Party time tonight.
No incidents, no trouble, no problems.
You good. It's good. It's all good.
Yo, it's the cockblocking bitch— I mean, Nubia. See you at Tammy's party.
That's the dyke trying to date Quisha? You worried?
You kidding me? Look at her. She's built like a truck.
Hahahahahaha!
It's good. You're still good.
And it'd feel good to dogwalk that asshole.
H-hey... Nubia.

H-hey! Hi.
How's...it going?
Good! Good.
For now...
Oh, *this* is Nubia!
OOF!
He's told us so much about you.
He told, he *told!* Of course he told, oh shit, I'm so screwed...
Been talking about you nonstop for weeks.
No I—
All good things, we promise.
O-oh! That's... nice!
...Whet?

You the same Nubia that hangs with Jason Russel?
Yup.
Cool, I play soccer with him. He said you guys were at the E.Z. Shoppe that got robbed the other day. That's wild.
Oh! Y-yeah. We left before anything went down, though... thankfully.
Oscar was there, too. Saw the whole thing, right?
Did he...
I hope you're okay.
I'm fine, actually. Never had a gun pointed at me before, so that shook me a little, but...
Luckily someone showed up to save the day.
GABBY McNeill 4 PREZ
He won't tell us *who* though.

Afraid I didn't see nothing. Dudes robbing the place made us lie facedown on the ground.
Oh...oh wow...
That's what we said!
I think it was a girl, though? The clerk described her to the cops.
She sounded cute.
BRRRRIIIIINNG
Whoa, uhm...wow! That's...a lot! And we missed it! Me, Jason, Quisha, m-me.
Gotta go, class.
It was nice talking to you!

Wait, Nubia!
GO
sign up
ICHS
Are you going to Tammy's party?
Yeah! Yeah, I'm going with Quisha. I'm her "date" so some jerk will leave her alone.
That's cool, looking out for your friend. You a real protector type, huh?
You...could say that.
TRIG
I'll be there, too. Save me a dance?
That's corny as hell.
But okay... I will.
TRIG

The hell is Oscar playing at?

And are we really gonna pretend like he didn't look me dead in the eye after I smashed that dude with that A.T.M.?
Nubia! Dinner!

Looks like he really ain't tell nobody. *Yet.*
Maybe I can get him by himself and see what he wants. There we go, that's the plan.
I'll do it at the party.

First I gotta *get* to the party.

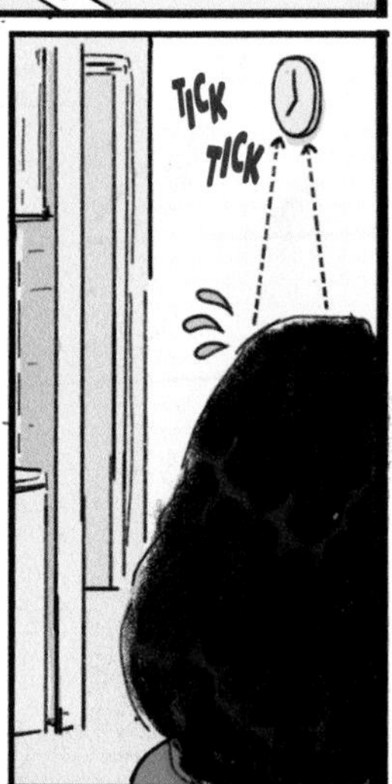
TICK
TICK

I can do this. I can *do* this.
I've punched out muggers. I took down *two* armed robbers. I got this.

TICK
TICK

I don't got this...

They're gonna eat me alive if I get caught.

Nubia, baby, are you okay?

Yes! Yes, ma'am.
I know you're likely still upset about this whole party thing...
Grk.
But we love you. One day you'll look back and understand that's why we do any of this.

I know. I love you too.
I'm finished. May I be excused?
Of course, dear.
SCRUB SCRUB
STOMP
STOMP
STOMP
BANG
PLZ KNOCK
Have a kid, she said. It'll be easy, she said.
Actually, she said it'd likely be the most difficult, harrowing, and terrifying experience either of us would ever know.
And simultaneously the best thing that ever happened to us.

Deep breath.
You got this.
You *got* this!

Good night.
Bed already?
It's been a long week, and I'm tired.

Okay, then. Love you, Nubs.
Love you, baby.
Love you guys.

Whew...

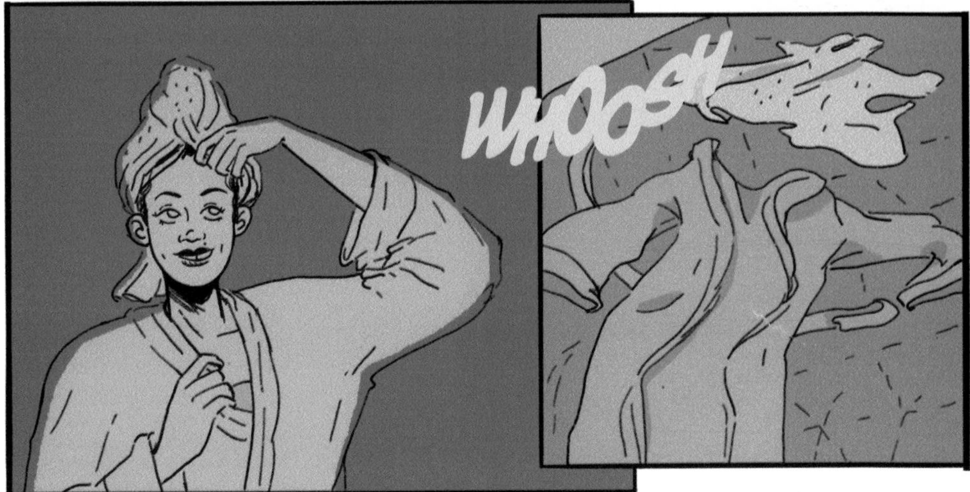
WHOOSH

We here.
Tell her where "here" is, fool. We on Roswell.
Hurry up, she's texting me insults while we sitting in the same car. Black Audi, BTW.
Fancy. OMW.

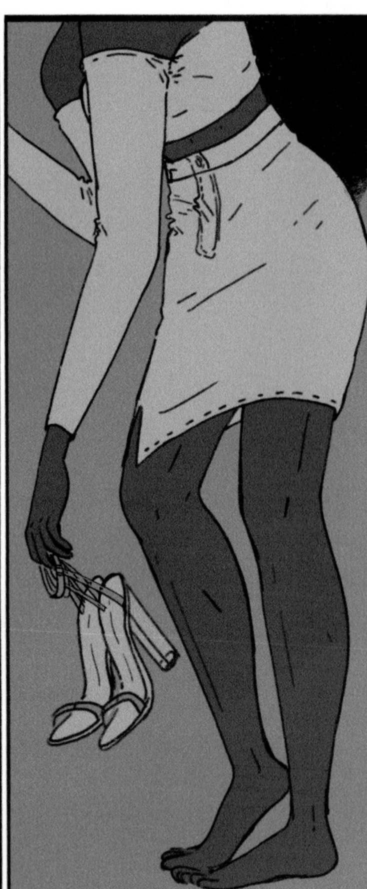

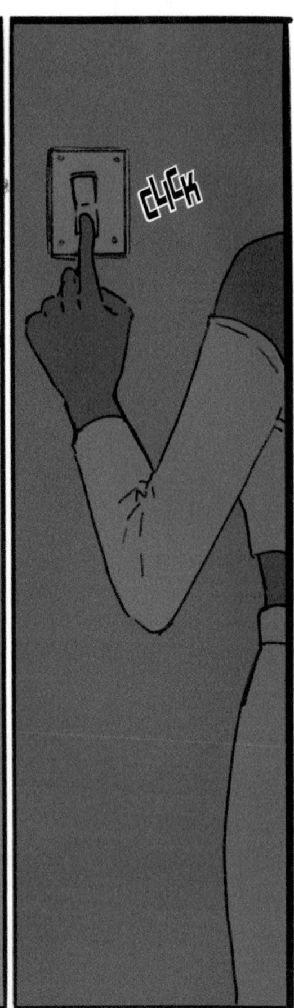
CLICK

I'm really 'bout to do this.
I can't ***believe*** I'm 'bout to do this.
I better hurry up and do this before I punk out.

Gah!
CRASH
MRRROW!
Sorry, kitty!

Damn, girl!

Your mommas let you out looking like a whole snack? 'Bout to drive 'em wild.

You *know* they didn't! Hurry up!

Hey! Nice car.
My mom's. Borrowed it so we could ride in style. Speaking of moms, you sure it's a good idea to test yours like this?
Whose side you on here?

The side of not gettin' my ass beat. If her moms find out I had anything to do with this, they'll tell my folks, then it's a wrap.
I'll take full blame, say y'all didn't know nothing. I'm already spending the summer alone. So what if it's in my room?

Well, if it's your last night of freedom...
Let's turn up!

And a *lot* of phones...

Now *this* is a party.

Am I drawing too much attention to myself? Maybe the heels were a bad idea...

What you mean?

I'm already a giant, now they make me...huge. I'm like an Amazon in these things.

Nothing wrong with that. Tall girls is where it's at.

I mean, that's what I hear.

That so?

F-from the guys on the team. I don't care. Tall, short...

Hey, you good?
Yeah, just... nervous, I guess.
Sneaking out, parties... never done this before.

It's cool. You need a minute to get acclimated.
Let's go get acclimated to some dranks!

For real, though, we got you. Just try and have some fun, yeah?
Fun...okay. That's a normal human emotion. I can do that.

I know you can. And we gon' do it with you!
WOOOOOOO!

Bab
k

Told you it would be fun!
Not gonna lie, the number of bodies freaked me out.
And the number of cameras, but so far so good.
It is wall-to-wall in here. Good food, though.

Thanks for bringing me. And not letting me chicken out.

Of course! You know we got your back.

Yeah, we wouldn't just abandon you or nothing.
MYMBLE

Hey, everything okay?
Fine! Everything's fine. I'm fine. Ahem
Oh, you fine, all right.

Let's get you a refill.
Whoa! I'm good, unless you spill it!
Then let's get *me* a drink. Nubia's got some unfinished business to handle.
W-w-wait, wait, what?

You got this!
Can you *not?!*
I believe in you!

I got this. O-okay. I got this.

Just walk up to him, ask him what his deal is.

He saw you throw an A.T.M., he won't try you.

Just kill me now...

Hey!
Hey, you made it.
I said I'd be here.
I'm glad.

Talk. To. Him.
Thanks? I'm glad you're here, too.
I actually need to talk. You. Talk *to* you! Weneedtotalk. *Ahem*

So, about that—
I almost didn't make it tonight.
Huh?
Between choir practice, homework, and my abuelita's birthday—she celebrates for the whole month—I'm beat! This is the longest week of my life.
How was your week?
Is he playing with me?
Stressful, if I'm being honest.
I'm sorry to hear that. Really...
But hey! You're here, right? Still standing. That's what's important.
And I remember you promising to save me a dance.
Maybe...maybe he's really gonna be cool about this...
Right. A dance.
A promise is a promise, I guess.

Ow!

S-sorry! It's these damn shoes.
I knew I shouldn't've worn th—

Don't take them off.
I think they look nice. You look nice. I-I...said that already, didn't I?

You did. But I like hearing it...
Wanna grab a drink?

You come to a lot of these things?
Not really. I'm not big on crowds.
Me neither.
I don't mind, though, especially with good company.
I'll let you know if I run into some.
H-hey!
The look on your face!
So now I'm funny lookin'?
I didn't say that!
First I'm not good company, now I got a weird face.
This is an attack.
Okay, now you being extra!

Hey, let's...can we find somewhere quiet? To talk.
O-okay.
I think it's pretty quiet outside.

Somewhere quiet, huh?
Just the two of us. Alone. Talking or whatever.

—this big!
That's what she said!
She did more than say it.

Can't wait for that asshole Wayland and his friends to graduate and get the hell out.
You and me both.

Come on, the stink of toxic masculinity filters out over here.

Ahem
So...
So.

I was hoping we could—
I'mnot kissingyouor whatever!

What—?
No! I mean... ugh, nothing! Never mind.
Pull yourself together, Johnson!
Uhm... okay...

I mean, don't go getting any ideas, with us being alone out here or...whatever.
What? No! Not at all! Not...not that you wouldn't be—that I wouldn't *want* to, but that's not—
I'm not— we...

Dios mio.
Let me start over.

I've been trying to figure out how to talk to you... about what happened at the E.Z. Shoppe? What...what I saw. What you did.
And what did you see? Think you saw. Maybe.

Something... pretty incredible. That I wouldn't mind seeing again, actually.
What, you want me to do a trick or something?

N-no! No. I-I didn't mean it like that.
I meant *you're* incredible, and I wanted to see you. Maybe talk.
Well, that's why we're here. So...talk.

I just figured it had to be hard, keeping a secret like that.
What?

And, I don't know, I just wanted to say...I'm here, I guess.
If you wanted to talk, I mean. More. Than now. Talking.

Just... talk.
Not blackmail me, or somehow make my life hell?
Yeah. About that or...anything, really.

I've been worried. You looked *so* scared when you bolted, and that woman tried to say you were involved.
But I told the cops she was wrong. That you—well, not *you*—but that girl? She saved us.
I just wanted to make sure you were okay. That's all.

So...you didn't tell anyone?

No.
Why...? Anyone else would be selling this story to TMZ to make a quick dollar.
Well...

I'd rather just get to know you. That'd be worth a lot more, at least to me.

I don't think that's a good idea.

"Opening up isn't...the best idea for me..."
Get out of here! Before I call the cops!

Messed-up shit happens, like with that clerk thinking I was trying to rob her.
People see what I can do and just... assume the worst.
I'm sorry.

You didn't do anything wrong. In fact, you're doing the most nothing ever, given the...situation.
I know. I'm still sorry people treat you like that.

Yeah, well. My moms say that's just how the world is. Wonder Woman saves the day, and it's a celebration. I save the day, and I end up in handcuffs.
Wait, handcuffs? You were arrested?

Almost. The cop eventually let me go, and I have you to thank for that.
Really. Thank you.
But... I don't wanna go through anything like that ever again.
I'm sorry.

That was pretty good, by the way. The line about getting to know me being worth more.
Yeah, well, I got a li'l game. But I mean it.

And I *am* sorry. Sucks that people overreact like that.
Me, too. But you deal, y'know?
Besides, it's been worse. I got caught on video once. Neglecting my surroundings, as Mama Amera calls it.

Clips started showing up online. We had to pack everything and move.
How many times have you had to do that?

I stopped counting at six.

Do Jason and Quisha know?
No... Just my parents.

That...that sounds really lonely.
It is...

But it'll never change, will it? I'll always be like this. Things will...always be like this.
I'm trapped...

Listen...this has been nice and all, but, uhm...I-I should go find my friends.

All right. And I meant it, when I said I wouldn't tell. I swear.

Thank you.

Hey! Wait, what's wrong?
Nothing.
This don't look like nothing.
I'm sorry for ruining things, but I'm...I'm over it, and I just...I want to go home.
Whoa, no problem. Really, it's good! We can go. Just need to grab Quisha.
Where is she?
They just refilled the fixings for s'mores, and she damn near broke her neck hurrying for the fire pit.
Oh no...

I swear to God, if Wayland...
Mmn!

Get off her!
What the hell—oh...
Are you okay?
I-I—
It's the dyke.
You need to mind your own business, bitch.
And you need to leave my friend alone.
Or what? Oh! Were you...hoping she would sleep with *you?*
I guess you're the next best thing to screwing a dude.
It was just a kiss. She's not complaining, so fuck off.
He's drunk, and you don't have to do this.
Would hitting you count as hitting a girl?
Try me, asshole.

WHOOSH
BIFF
SWOOSH

You...you think you're funny?
I'll show your monkey ass funny!

Did this asshole just—

Say it again.
What the hell?!
L-let me go!
Let me—
GRK!
Say.
It.
Again.

SNORT

That's what I thought.

WHACK

Yo, man, you good?
How many fingers am I holding up?
Oh no.

No no nonono no NO!
Hey...
You okay?
Nubia! Wait!
Nubia!

Stupid...
So stupid!

You let him get to you.
You let him, and now! Now...

Everyone saw.
EVERYONE.
Damn it, Nubia, how could you let it happen? Again...

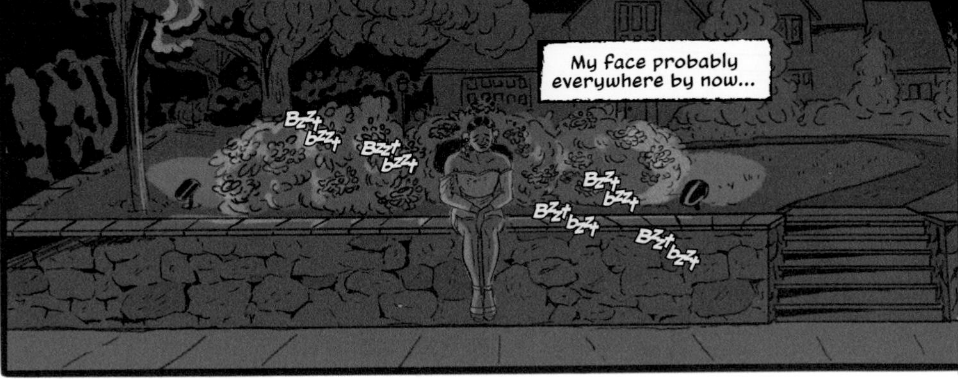
My face probably everywhere by now...
Bzzt bzzt
Bzzt bzzt
Bzzt bzzt
Bzzt bzzt
Bzzt bzzt

You in the car?
What's wrong? What happened?
Where are you?
He deserved it.
You okay?
Where did you learn to move like that?
Where did you learn to PUNCH like that?
Please just tell me you're okay.

I'm okay. Really. I just freaked out and had to get some air. Cool off. Y'all go ahead and go home, I'mma take the bus.
You sure? We can come get you.
I'm sure. I need a minute.
Okay. Text us soon as you get home.
I will.

That was legendary BTW.

Sniff
CRACK
This seat taken?

Well, not *that* seat. That one's busted.
But there's one on the other side that looks fine.
How...how did you find me?

This is gonna sound hella creepy, but... I followed you.
I just wanted to make sure you were okay.
Not, like, physically okay—clearly you can take care of yourself.
But that was a lot, and you were upset before, and just... are you okay?

I'm sorry, I'm talking too much. I should shut up.
No...no. You're fine. And thanks.
I'm okay. I think.

I can't believe I let that asshole bait me into—so stupid. I should know better.
That wasn't stupid. You knew the risks and took them anyway to protect someone.
So stupid *brave,* maybe.
Especially since no one else did anything.

No, they didn't. Not even you...
Yeah...
Why didn't you? You saw what he was doing. You were just gonna let it happen?

I...was waiting to see if anyone else would.
I wanted to. I tried to! But I was...
You were what?

Scared.

I got picked on when I was little. A lot. One bully in particular made my life hell.
Three guesses who.
Wayland.

Yup. Wayland and his friends tortured me all through middle school.
So when I made a move and they stopped me, telling me to quit cock-blocking, I froze.

Everyone talks about how Wayland's gotten away with murder since grade school.
You, Jason, Quisha. It's like y'all just accept him and his trash behavior. Like it's okay.

But it's not! ***Nothing*** about tonight was okay! None of the things he does are okay!
You're right. You're totally right. I'm sorry.

I'm not blaming ***you*** or nothing, but—
No. No, I get it. And I messed up. No matter the reason, I just stood there.
I'll do more next time. I promise.

Good.

I should get going. It's getting late and I'm pretty partied out.
Want me to walk you home? Or to wherever.
Not that you need protecting, I just...it'd be nice to...maybe...

Yeah. You can walk with me a bit.

How come nobody ever did anything about Wayland?
People's parents had to be pissed. Mine would be.
His parents are rich, and they know a lot of important people. I think there's a street named after his family.
No joke? What is it, Asshole Avenue?

Naw, I think it's Dickhead Drive.
Bitch-Ass Boulevard!

Puto Parkway.
Oh my god, stop!

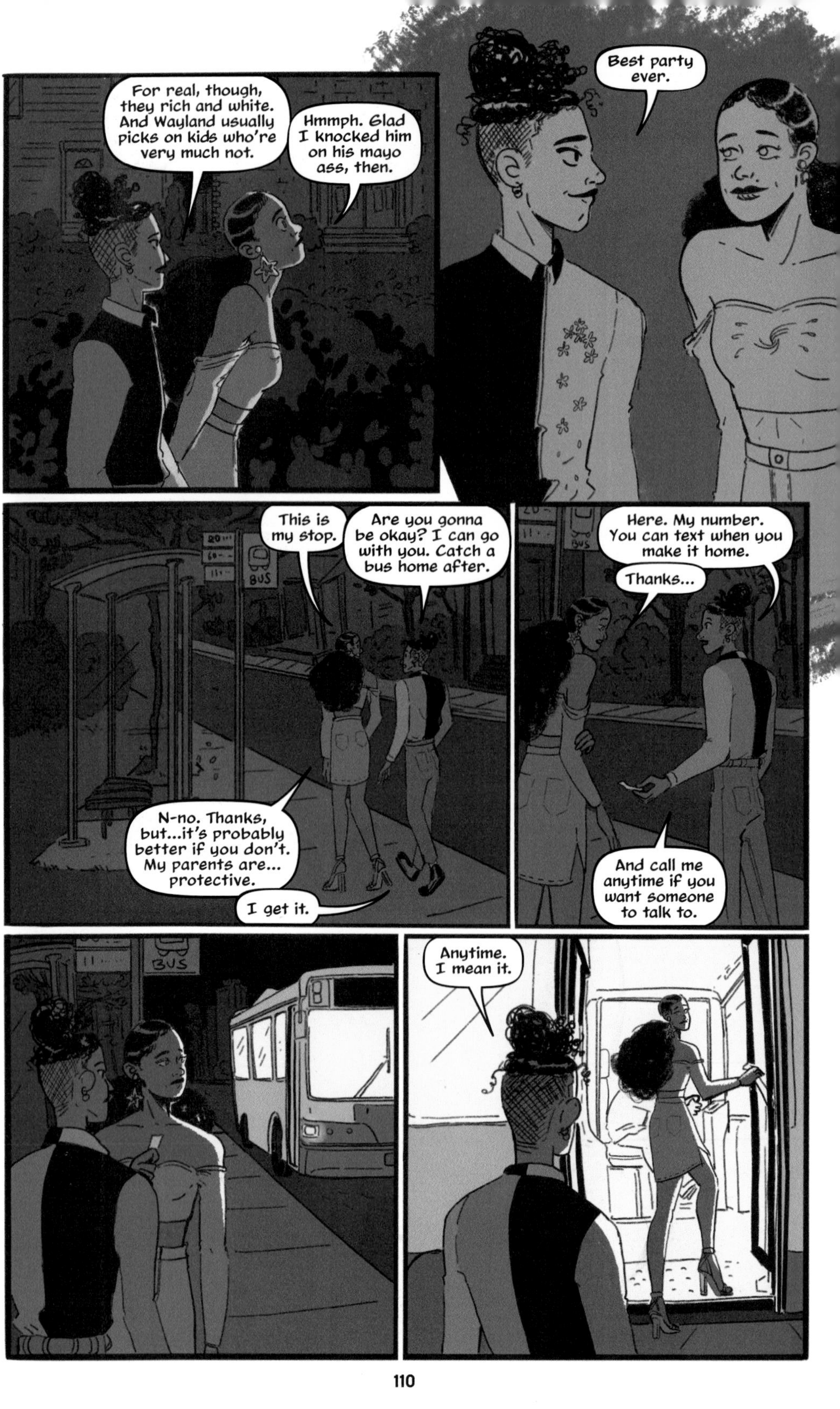

For real, though, they rich and white. And Wayland usually picks on kids who're very much not.
Hmmph. Glad I knocked him on his mayo ass, then.
Best party ever.

"I really wish you wouldn't do that..."
"Mm?"
"Switch channels back and forth."
"Babe...it's a commercial."

They're all commercials, so you may as well stay on the channel.
You're halfway asleep anyway, not even watching.
I can still hear you flipping.

I'm fine! You don't—
Aww hell.
Well...care to explain yourself?
Starting with why you're hanging from my drapes in what is definitely *not* your pajamas.
I—
...

You went to that party, didn't you?
After we explicitly told you not to.

...
I—
I'm sorry!
I'm sorry for everything...
I keep messing up.
I'm sorry I'm like this. I wish I wasn't!
I wish I wasn't **broken.**
I-I...I can't turn it off...I'm sorry you're stuck with me.
That you can't have a normal life. W-with a normal kid...
I'm sorry...

There isn't a damn thing wrong with you, you hear me?
Don't ever say that. Don't even think it. You are perfect, Nubia, exactly as you are.
The rest of the world is broken. Not you. Never you. You hear me?

SNIFF
Y-yes, ma'am.
Good. Now c'mere.

Now, was all this about you getting caught sneaking out? Because it seems like there's more going on...
Sigh

They're gonna find out. Or D will tell them about the videos... Better if it's me, I guess.
Kind of?

Quisha was trying to fight him, but...
12:01 AM

Well...little racist got what he deserved.
Wish you could've hit him twice.
He swung first, though.
12:33 AM

No one else tried to stop him? Why am I not surprised.
What do you mean?
1:17 AM

I mean this wasn't a robbery, it was a party. There was a room full of equally capable people. One of them could have done something, *should* have.
Everyone just sat there. Until I clocked him.
Again, he deserved it.
KDOT

You shouldn't always have to be the first to put yourself out there like that.
Now we're teaching our daughter to never look out for anyone but herself?

That's not at all what I—
There's nothing wrong with sticking up for the people you love.

I never said there was. But what happened at this party is exactly what we—
I know. But do we want her to feel like she can't stand up for herself?
Like she has to creep around hiding from everyone and everything? From *life?*
Life is dangerous, Danielle.
I ***know.*** It's also beautiful and amazing, and she deserves a chance to live it.
She won't get that chance if she's not careful. They'll take it from her.
Like they took that boy Quentin's.
Like they'll take someone else's tomorrow.
So, what, she's a recluse the rest of forever? ***We*** lock her up? "For her own good"?
Where is this coming from? We're not doing that. She's not a prisoner.
No? She's lying to us. Sneaking out.
Ma-maybe we're smothering her.
We need to adjust.
We have a plan, Danielle. We swore.
Plans change! Or they should. What kind of
ents tell their child not
o what's right?!
It's not that simple.
It seems simple to me!
at if someone
alled the police?
hey show u
the Black
unching
white b
hat happens then? You
think they stop to ask
ho was right or wron
They don't care
bout that. They jus
pull the trigger.
Nubia needs to look out for herself. No one else will.

WE WILL!

But we might not be enough...

Maybe...maybe it's time to call in some professional help.
Professional help? The hell does that mean?

She said emergencies. I think this counts.
Are you sure?
What, is there, like, a hotline for a super-powered child psychologist or something?

Not exactly.

Hey, D. We have a situation.
Does she *have* to call me a situation?
She's calling the situation a situation, dear. Now get some rest.

≈Sigh≈
That went well.
Freaking D has more of a say in my life than I do, and we ain't never even met...

Yo, you good?
Nubia, where are you?
Answer. Quisha's freaking out.
Nubia?

BLERP

Where'd I put that...

OSCA
678-999-8

# PART III

I thought I might find you here.
I came to enjoy the view.
Beautiful...
The view's not bad either.
You wouldn't say that if you knew what I am.
But I do. And you wouldn't doubt me if you could see yourself how I see you.
Let me look at you...Nubia...
Mm?
Nubia!
Nubia! Get up! Breakfast is ready!

omg

Local Boy Attacked at Party

OMG!! Nubia, what's happening?

Wow, girl, w/e happened 2 takin the high road?

@NubiaJ_03 He 1000% deserved it!!!

Your parents see?

PicStagram

J_Olsen40

J_Olsen40: K.O.!

comments :

Are you okay?

**Teenager Assaulted by Classmate**

Yuptoob

Do you have a plan?

You need to get a lawyer or something!

anonymous :
@NubiaJ_03 WHAT ARE YOU ?

Tall, Dark, and...Dangerous? Click link to read article

Y-you... you're...

Hello, Nubia, it's nice to see you. I'm Diana.

Oh. My. Gawd.

Wonder Woman knows my name!

I know much more than that.

Wonder Woman's in my ***HOUSE!***

Wait...Wonder Woman's in my house—why is Wonder Woman in my house?
Sit down, baby. We need to talk to you.
All of us.
This...this isn't how we wanted you to find out.
We hoped it would be a celebration.
Something planned and happy instead of...a result of this nonsense.
Benes
Wait...is this the "you're adopted" talk? 'Cuz we had that when I was, like, six.
It is, but it isn't. At least, not in the typical way.
I know you've been having trouble dealing with unusual things cropping up in your life.
Your superhuman abilities being one of them.
Benes
It's not... I mean... yeah...
But I didn't expect my moms to call in freaking Wonder Woman.
And I'm sure you've been wondering what gave you these powers. What makes you who you are. What you are.
Y-yes.

The reason you're having trouble passing as human is... because you're not. Human, that is.
You're an Amazon, Nubia.
You're my twin sister.

I...wait, WHAT?!
Try to remain calm.

Th-that's not possible!
I know this is hard to believe.

No, I mean it's not possible 'cause you're, like, a million years old!
No offense...

I-I don't mean... just...how is this possible?
We were born at the same time. Though "born" is not exactly how I would describe it.

Look, if I'm some kinda pod person, I'm done.
No, you're—that's not—let me explain...

"We were molded together, by her hand and her heart, and with her love."
"Her?"
"Our mother, Hippolyta, queen of the Amazons. She then prayed we would be given life.
BOOM
"Mother often told me we were the greatest blessing she ever received.
"But tragedy struck in the form of Ares...
"...the god of war."

HALT!
"You were believed to be lost.
"It wasn't until decades later that I discovered one of Ares's abandoned strongholds.
"He had been defeated in battle, and I wanted to ensure he could not pose any future threat.
"Instead...
"...I found you."

"We don't know what he had planned for you, but there you were.
"Ares had placed you in a suspended state, halting your aging.
"I took you back to Themyscira, to Mother.
"Finding you was a miracle we had long thought impossible, but it was bittersweet...
"Having left the island, though not by choice, you could not remain."

Mother still wanted you to be raised by an Amazon. Me, actually.
But my duties would only be a danger to you.
Yet there was another way.

"I brought you to the home of one of my sisters.
"An Amazon who had found love during a mission in the world of men and decided to stay.
SOLD

It was agreed she and her love would raise you, teach you, protect you as their own.

Wait...
Wait! You for real?!

This is...I can't... my mom is an immortal warrior?
I wouldn't say immortal.

And...I'm an... **Amazon?**
Yes. An Amazon ***princess,*** to be exact.
A princess. A ***PRINCESS.*** Oh my god...

Wh-why...why didn't you ***tell*** me any of this?!
So you could decide what you wanted to do with your life.
Plus the whole sworn-to-secrecy thing.

I promised I would look in on you from time to time, but I would not interfere with whatever path you chose for yourself.
That you would be allowed to grow into your own person. And for the most part, I have kept that promise.
We ***all*** only wanted what was best for you. We still do. That's why I'm here now.

We told Diana about the situation concerning this... Wayland and the media.
There has been more than one occasion when the media turned against members of the Justice League.
So I know, ***somewhat,*** what you're experiencing, but I will never fully understand what you're going through.
And while none of it is your fault, you have a choice to make.
You can leave, like before. Start over in another city, another country even.
But you may inevitably be discovered down the road.
Or you can stay, even though who and what you are may not be a secret much longer.
This is your home. You have a right to be here. And to do what makes you feel safe.
Asking that you make this decision, so soon after learning the truth of your birth, is a lot, but ask I must.
Before you choose, I want you to know I will support you and do my part to guide and train you. I am here for you, my sister.

I need...to think. About everything.
Of course. This has to be your decision. We can't make it for you. Understand?

Y-yes... *Sniff*
Good. And just know, no matter what you decide, it will be the right choice.
O-okay.

Now, I have one more thing for you.

Mother and I made these. For you. You are an Amazon, a warrior. Use them wisely. Wear them with honor...
Mother would be proud to see you as you are today.
Bene's

"Be well,
little sister."

The protest set to take place this afternoon is supposed to be a peaceful one—

But police have already begun to gather in the area.

Hey. Come get me on your way to the park.
Wait, you comin?
Yes.
Ayyyyyyy
Yo!

Benes

The crowd has grown to at least a few hundred people, and more are arriving every minute.

JUSTICE

This is a community that has clearly had enough.

And where do you think you're going?

The protest. Quisha's been planning it for weeks.

Are you sure you—

It's gonna be peaceful, mostly a bunch of kids.

People don't really see Black and brown kids as kids.

I know. Which is why we're doing this. *So* they see us.

I'd like to be there, to support my friend.

And... maybe...kinda sorta baby-step into the hero thing?

After today, whatever you eventually decide, we support you.
Thanks, Mom...
HONK
HONK

You be careful!
I will be. I promise.
Get something to eat first, something light!
Okay. I love you guys.

Wait!

M-Mom?

Turn off location on your phone so they can't track you.
Make sure you have an exit strategy for if things pop off, and a designated rendezvous point.
If there's any pepper spray, use milk, not water, to wash it off.
Eyes. Nose. Throat. That's what you go for first.

I'm so *proud* of you...

It's cool your moms are letting you do this.
After that video popped up on the news? I just **knew** we was never gonna see you again.
Yeah, I know. Guess...they changed their minds.
And I guess a conversation with ***Wonder Woman*** will do that.
NO JUSTICE NO PEACE

You never did tell us where you learned to throw hands like that.
You taking classes or something?
And what're y'all gonna do about the media? Wayland out here lying his ass off about what happened.
Pops said y'all should sue for libel or defamation or whatever.

Don't worry about me, I'm not the one Wayland pushed up on.
You okay, Quisha? You been checking on me this whole time, but...

I'm good, I guess. Mostly.
And by "mostly" you mean...
I mean, my mom wants me to file assault charges, but...

With everything blowing up, that might just make things worse for you.
Didn't I say don't worry about me? Wayland shouldn't keep getting away with this.
So if you wanna say something, you say something.
Or if you want something more, we can do that too.

And what *you* mean?
I *mean* me and Nubia can tune his ass up. Be hard for him to kiss people with a broke jaw.
Much as I would pay to see that, it'll just get y'all in even more trouble.

And much as I would *love* to sleep that fool—
Again.
*Again...*I can't afford the extra attention right now.

I ain't try'na be that guy, but what happened to "Don't worry about me"?
Nothing. But Quisha pressing charges and us jumping him are two different things.
One is about fighting for the truth. The other is just fighting.

Which I'm cool with, just not right now. You **know** they'll twist it. They already are...

Aight, I hear you. Charges now, ass-whuppin's later.
Sounds like a plan.

Thanks, y'all. For real.
I got you.
NO JUSTICE
NO PEACE
NO RACIST
POLICE

I mean we! **We** got you. Both of us. Nubia and me...
We sure do.
NO JUSTICE
NO PEACE
NO RACIST
POLICE

I gotta check in with the other organizers. Be right back!

NEWS

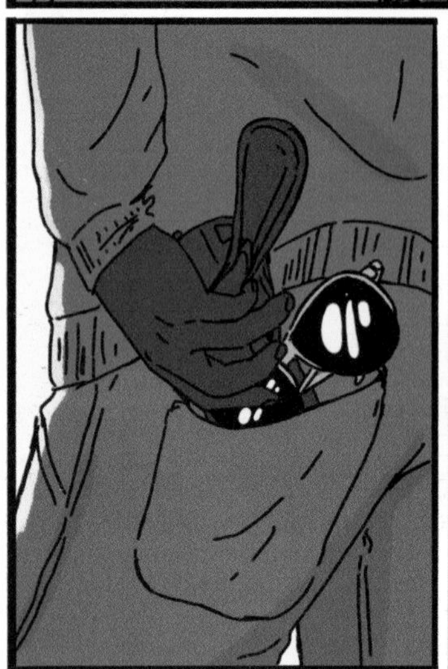

Okay, what's this?
What's what?
Your...disguise. That what that's s'posed to be?
I don't wanna draw attention to myself.

Right, because nothing is less suspect to white people than somebody Black trying to look inconspicuous.
Boy, you can't even spell "inconspicuous"!
Everything is set. Let's get our stuff and get out there.

What's so funny?
Nubia thinks she's a spy.
Don't make me hurt you.

Let's hurry, they're waiting for—
Quisha!
Great...
STO
POLI
BRU
BLAC
LIVES
MATTER
OTECT
R
REN

4
NEWS
Okay, now he's ***looking*** to get faded.
Easy.
Though you right. This is ballsy.
ACK

Hey, listen, last night? We both had a little too much to drink and some signals were mixed up.
Mixed signals? I wasn't—
It was a party and people were partying. It was kind of wild.
Is this your half-assed way of apologizing?

The past is the past.
It was twelve hours ag—
Let's focus on today.
Wayland, I'm busy, and I ain't got time for you or your nonsense. Why you even here?

To make sure you didn't have the wrong idea about last night. And... the cause.
Tuh!
The shithead cause, you mean.

It doesn't matter. I don't want you here.
Why not? I apologized.
Because you're a pushy, sexist, phobic, *racist* bully, and that wasn't an apology.
I'm *not* racist.

You called Nubia a monkey!
That wasn't— that was the liquor, not me!
Uh-huh. I should've told you off a long time ago.
Take your bum ass on somewhere and leave me alone.
NO JUST

Y-y-you! You don't talk to me like—!

You better rethink that.
And think hard.
Don't be stupid. There's three of us.
You sure about that, playboy?
Whatever. I'm not even into Black chicks, just wanted to nail one to say I did.
Figured your fat ass was low-hanging fruit.
NEWS

You need to walk away before I give you a matching set.
You're gonna get yours, bitch.
All of you. Every last fucking one.
Grade A asshole, man.
Screw him. Let's get ready.
I don't like this.
Nubia!

Oscar?!
Hey, folks.
What...are you doing here?
STOP KILLING Black Trans Women

I planned on doing this since Quisha handed out flyers last week.
JUSTICE 4 Quentin
AQTA
That's what's up.

You okay? There's a lotta cops here. Lotta news, too.
I'm good. Keeping my head down, y'know.
It'll be okay. We're with you.
Thanks...
AQTA

Okay, y'all! Let's do this! Everybody say JUSTICE!
JUSTICE!
NO JUSTICE
NO PEACE
NO RACIST
*Man,* you corny...

LIVES MATTER
CHILDREN
NO JUSTICE NO PEACE NO RACIST POLICE
LIVES MATTER
NO JUSTICE
FTP
QUENTIN
NO MORE
DONT SHOOT
PROTECT OUR CHILDREN
POLICE
POLICE
POLICE
BLACK TRANS LIVES MATTER

Who will Keep us SAFE?
Network
IS MY SON NeXT?!
MY LIFE

PROTECT OUR children
JUSTICE 4 Quentin
BLACK LIVES MATTER
IS MY SON NEXT?
NO MORE KILLER COPS
JUSTICE
This is amazing! There are at least five hundred people here.
Probably more. You're amazing for putting this together.
I had help...
What was that?
Can't really tell from back here.
CRASH
NO JUSTICE NO PEACE NO RACIST

Come on.

POLICE
Mierde.
JUSTICE 4
NO MORE KILLER COPS
STOP KILLING Black Trans Women
That's not good.
No, the cops aren't even supposed to be here. We have a permit!

Gimme a boost.
Here, careful.
I got you.

I know this looks scary, but we have done nothing wrong.
We have a right to protest peacefully. We have a right to be heard. We have a right to make them listen!
Everybody stay calm. Look after each other. Stay smart. Stay safe.

You think there's gonna be any trouble?
Not from us. Hopefully they feel the same way.

POLICE
POLICE
SMACK
Cease and desist immediately or you will be dispersed.
Where's it coming from?!
Please, stop!
Something's not right.
Black lives matter!
Fuck the police!
Fascists!

Pow.

IS MY CHILD NEXT?

WE NEED JUSTICE!

STOP THIS

BLACK LIVES MATTER

NO MORE KILLER COPS

KSSH

POLICE

POLICE

No...

CE
NO MORE KILLER COPS
We have to go!
NO RACIST
POLICE

Freeze!
Hands in the air!
NO JUSTICE
NO PEACE
NO RACIST
POLICE
Now!
Put down the weapon!

Sugar Shack
W-weapon? I don't have a—
Put it down!
CLOSED
JUSTICE NOW
I-it's not a weapon.
Put it down! NOW!
I-I'll show you! It's not a weapon, look!

AHH!!!

Nngh!
H-he...
Get on the ground!
...he jumped in front of it...
He jumped...
You shot him!
Why are you doing this? We didn't do anything!
NO JUSTI NO PEAC NO RACIST POLICE
ON THE GROUND!
Danielle said put pressure on wounds.
Move away from—
Nnnnnnn!
A-and... tourniquet. I- I need a—
Help him.

Stop shooting us!
Stop shooting us!
Get your hands up and back away from the suspect!
NO JUSTICE NO PEACE NO RACIS POLIC
You have to help him!
Four suspects in custody, one injured. Send backup.
STOP SHOOTING US!
STOP RESISTING!
"Kids like us get shot."
"You tried to crush my baby, you *freak!*"
"One misstep and they crucify you.
"People don't really see Black and brown kids as kids."
"I know. Which is why we're doing this..."

So they see us.

*What the—?*

SMACK!

*Hnng!*
*Ahh!*
I got you, hey, I got you.
We gotta go, ***now!***

GILBERT MEMORIAL HOSPITAL
EMERGENCY
EMERG

Police are trying to quell what is now a full-on riot, which started as a peaceful protest.

The protest was organized in response to a police-involved shooting of a young Black man just last week.

There are reports of shots fired in the area, and at least two casualties.
Breaking News: Riots in McArthur Park
WPN

NO JUSTIC
NO PEACE
NO RACIS

CLICK

# PART IV

BZZ
bzz
bzz

SQUAD
How y'all doing?
Not good. I can't believe that happened...
I know. WTF?
Did you sleep?
No. Nightmares.
It's all over the class board. They're looking or suspects who ttacked some cops.

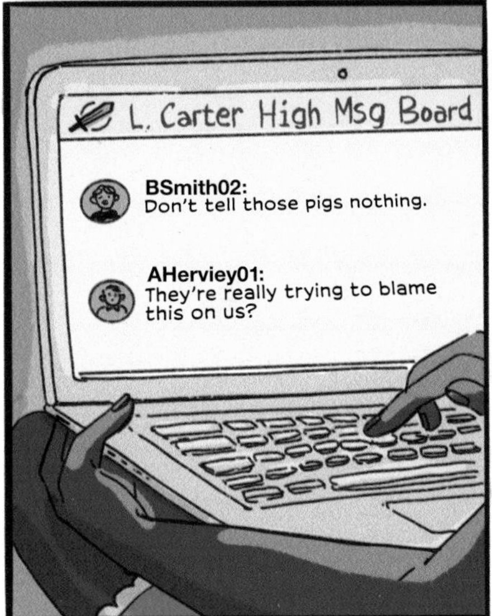
L. Carter High Msg Board
BSmith02:
Don't tell those pigs nothing.
AHerviey01:
They're really trying to blame this on us?

BSmith02:
PREACH.
WCarson01:
I knew this "protest" was a bad idea. Just people looking to blame someone for the crime in their community.
WCarson01:
Someone should do something about these dangerous thugs before they hurt innocent people. I'll do it if no one else will.
SEmerson01:
You know who did this, Wayland?
WCarson01:
Damn straight, and I'm not going to let them get away with it. Especially the one who started all this.

Uggggghhhhh, that motha!

Nubia?
I brought some breakfast.
No thanks.
You need to try and eat something.

I ate something.
Something that's not a dozen cookies. Come on.
Cookies

There.

Sigh
About what happened at the protest...

If it wasn't for Wayland and his racist-ass friends...!
Ahem

Sorry. I just...
*They* started things with the police—the actual protesters didn't do anything!

People like Wayland are dangerous.
They're used to getting their way, no matter who gets hurt.
A lot of the time, they do the hurting.

First Quisha. Now Oscar...
And he's gonna get away with it.
Unless...
Unless?

I-I...I don't know how to stop this, without...
Or if I even can. Or if I should try.
I'll probably just make things worse.
Nubia. I know I say you should be careful because of how the world perceives you...
But that perception is their problem, not yours.
All these years I've been trying to protect you from this nonsense...
Perhaps I should've done more to prepare you for it.
You prepared my right hook.
*Ha!* We'll work on your follow-through.
Baby... none of this is fair.
Not Wayland. Not the cops. Not having to hide who you are, or deal with people who would likely set themselves on fire if it meant watching you burn.

More importantly, none of it is *your* fault.
I'm sorry if I ever made it sound like you were responsible for anyone but yourself.
You didn't. I-I just...I wish it wasn't like this.

Me, too, baby.
One more thing.

I know yesterday was a lot.
And I know I've told you to hide who you are.
*And* I still worry about what could happen, but I found these in the trash and, well–

I was wrong.

Not about people feeling threatened by you or trying to weaponize the parts of you they can't control, because that will still happen...
But how you handle it is up to you.

And don't you let anyone make you feel like you need to throw pieces of yourself away to be part of this world.
You be you. All of you, all the time. Everyone else will deal with it.
Thanks, Mom.
Knock knock. Hey, baby. Just got a call from Oscar's grandma.
He's out of surgery. Can't have any visitors yet. Maybe tomorrow.
Sure...If he even wants to see me...
Why wouldn't he? You saved his life. He'll probably call you a hero.
I don't feel very heroic.
True heroes seldom do.

He's okay. That's what matters.

He's...he's okay.
CLICK
Officers say the altercation began when protesters started throwing debris, including bricks and bottles.
A number of arrests have been made, but no details on individual charges were released.

This isn't my fault. This. Isn't. My. Fault.
An investigation into the shooting of a minor is—
Click

Hey, Oscar...How are you?
How are you feeling?
Are you okay?
I'm sorry I haven't called.
Or visited.
I'm sorry...
Click
Click
Click
Click
Click
Click
DELETE

Sigh

I'll...call tomorrow.

"Nubia, breakfast is on the table."

"Coming!"

MAMA BEAR

Hey, if you're not ready to face school today, that's okay.

I could call in, say you're not feeling well.

Thanks, but I wanna go.

I don't wanna sit up there just...

Replaying what happened in my head...

If you say so. But the second you don't feel up to it, call us.

You still haven't been to see Oscar, have you?
No...I mean, what if he blames me for—
It wasn't your fault.
I know. But you know how people can be.
Not Oscar, he's *good* peoples. He wouldn't do nothing like that.
We should go visit after school. Together.
I'm down.
Maybe...
Someone said it was some gang stuff.
If I was his family, I'd sue.
You can't sue a gang.
They're talking about Oscar.
I know.
His family *should* sue. That cop shot him!
But that ain't how the media will tell it.
However they tell it, I'm part of it now...
However they tell it, we gotta make sure they keep Nubia out of it.
Wait, what? I thought you said—
Oscar won't blame you, but these fools might.
You know how they do.

The cops haven't shown up at your house, right?
That means they don't know it was you who laid 'em out. And we gotta keep it that way.

We figured we could be witnesses for Oscar, but we just say we don't know you.
That way, they can focus on the shooting and not that well-deserved ass-whuppin'.

Wow. Thanks, guys.
But I'd never ask you to lie like that for me.
Good thing you didn't ask.

Hold on...!

When was y'all gonna tell me about this?
It's not... I mean...!
She's making it weird. Don't make it weird.

BRRRRRIIIIINNNNNGGGG!
Lemme just say FI-NAL-LY!
Girl, shut up. We'll see you at lunch.

I can't let them lie like that, can I?
I mean, what if someone finds out?
Then we all get in trouble...

Mama Danielle said an investigation will show that it was a cop's bullet that hit Oscar.
Mama Amera said that won't make a difference if they don't want it to...

Ugh! This is all Wayland's fault!
I swear, when I see him I'mma reach down his throat and—
Code red! This is not a drill! Lockdown! Lockdown!
What?
Oh my god...
Test Today!
BULLETIN
Wait, what's happening?!
Active shooter alert, this is not a drill!

click

SHOVE
SVU

I have to do something.
SVU

I have to...

I-I...

What if the shooter gets me first?

What if they think ***I'm*** the shooter...

I can't... I'm not...

Holy shit, it's Wayland!
The shooter is Wayland Carson!
What?!

Michelle just saw him by the gym, he's got a gun! She posted a pic.

Let me see!
Not so loud!

L. Carter High Msg Board
SEmerson01:
You know who did this, Wayland?
WCarson01:
Damn straight, and I'm not going to let them get away with it. Especially the one who started all this.
Oh no...

Quisha!
???
Nubia!
WOOSH
SMACK
CLUB
JOIN TODAY
MCNEILL 4 PREZ
Physics TUTOR?
Winter Musical audition sign up
Troy
Gabriella

Lock it behind me!
NO! WAIT!

SLAM

Have to find her, before he does.
Second period. Study hall.
Hurry...

He doesn't know her schedule.
He can't know it. Oh my god, if something happens to her...
HURRY!

Library→
I'm too late...

You don't get to say no to me. **NOT** you!
SILENCE IS GOLDEN
READ
Ah!
SMACK

Nubia, RUN!
WOOSH
BANG!
Relax & Read

Nnng!
Not bulletproof. Not bulletproof!
N-Nubia?
T-told you... I got your back.
What... how...you're a-a supe-super–?!
Yes...no...it's complicated.
I knew it!
I knew your butch ass was some kinda freak!
⫸Tsss⫷
Oh my god!
I'm fine. Not as bad as it looks.
Go. I can handle him, but not if I have to worry about you!
I'm not leaving you! What if—
I've got this, Quisha. I'm stronger than him. Faster. I'll be all right.
I'm going to show everyone what you really are!

There's only one way out, and it's through me!
Y-you better be. I love you.
I love you, too.
BANG
BANG
BANG
GO! NOW!
BANG
Coward!
I'm not the one running, am I? See if you can punch me now.
You still feeling fragile? Poor baby.
Not smart to insult the man with the gun.

Man? You're just some li'l boy who couldn't handle losing a fight to a girl.
So you whip out a gun to feel better about yourself.
Shut up...
Do strong girls scare you, Wayland?
I bet you're terrified.
I said shut up!
That why you try to intimidate them? And when that doesn't work, you hurt them. Like Maria.
Maria didn't know her place. None of you bitches do. You need reminders.
Broken bones and bullets?
Whatever gets the job done.
BANG
BANG
BANG
You can't even stop shaking long enough to aim straight.
You think I'm scared of you? You're nothing. ***NOTHING.***
Just ghetto trash that needs to be cleaned up, and everyone's gonna see.

Whenever you're in trouble, take a moment to ground yourself. Remeber to breathe. Stay in the now.

I got video of you attacking those cops at the protest.

I know it's tough, but whatever decision you make is the right one.

I'll be the hero who stopped you before you really hurt someone.

You, then your cocktease friend.
We're with you. Always.

That's not what happened, and you know it.
That's what they'll see, and that's all that matters.
When I'm done, no one's going to believe a word you say.

Besides... bodies don't talk.

What...?
How...?
When I'm done, no one's going to believe—
—a word you say.
Not this time, asshole.
No...
BANG

CRASH
Oomph!

Someone's going viral.

Bzz
bzz
bzz
bzz
bzz
bzz
Looks like the only one exposed here is you.
W-wait. Wait, no, this isn't...this isn't right...

No...
Y-you can't do this to me...
You did this to yourself!

Y-you can't... Not you. *Never you!*

BANG
CLINK
SMACK
Aagh!
I warned you'd get a matching set.

Students and teachers at L. Carter High are still reeling from a shooting earlier this afternoon.
Reports of alleged harassment and assault perpetrated by the shooter, who is now in police custody, have begun to surface.
NEWS AT NINE

There are also reports of a young woman possessing superhuman abilities, who stepped in to neutralize the shooter before police were able to arrive on the scene. They say this girl's actions likely saved the lives of her fellow students, making her a hero.
SUPASONIC

I'm so proud of you.
Even though I'm...not much of a secret anymore?
You're here. You're safe. And you stopped something terrible from happening. We'll handle anything else that comes up.

I wasn't *trying* to be a hero, I just...I knew he was going after Quisha, and I had to stop him.
People who *try* to be heroic seldom are. When you step up like that, it requires all of you.
Defend the ones you love with your whole heart and every breath. That is the Amazon way.

You gonna teach me how to be an Amazon now?
A lesson or two can't hurt.

Hey, Nubs, you up for some company?
Company?

These two have been chomping at the bit to see you, it seems.

O-oh! Hey! Yeah!
Quisha said you saved her life!
I also said it was a secret, dodo bird. Don't you be listening?

I'm sure her **moms** know!
I can't take you anywhere.

We need to go sign some paperwork. You kids gonna be okay?
Yes, ma'am.
Call us if you need anything.
Jason, don't touch my cookies.
COOKIE
I'll make sure he behaves.
Some clean clothes are in the duffel, Nubs. Change anytime you're ready.
Okay.
So, you're a for-real superhero, huh? Like, in real life and stuff.
Heh, yes, in real life.
That's soooooo dope! You got a cool name?

What's wrong with Nubia?
Ain't nothing wrong with Nubia! But heroes have names!
Batman! Superman! Wonder Woman!

How 'bout... Bad Bitch.
My moms would *kill* me.
I know, I'm just playing.

...
Thank you. ***Thank you.***
And not just for me. For Maria, and everyone he ever hurt.
People coming forward talking about all the bullshit his family covered up. He's done!

I...never imagined this could happen. Thank you. ***Thank you.***
Thank *you* for being amazing. What you did filming those cops? Inspired me.

Now...everyone will know the truth.

You a real one, Nubia.
The realest. And my best friend.

Who my best friend?
That's my best friend!
KNOCK
KNOCK
KNOCK

Your moms can't be done *that* quick.
Can you get the door, Jason?
Sure.

'Sup, folks.
Oscar!

You're okay!
I've had worse.
Ha! When?

I was so worried about y—

Ahem
So...

Everyone, this is my grandma. Abuelita, this is Quisha, Jason, and...
Nubia.
Nice to meet you, ma'am.

This is Nubia? Well, hello, Nuuuubia. This is the one you like, yes?
Okay! You met everyone! You should go get that coffee you wanted.
She has such good manners.
Oy...
And she's so lovely. You like my grandson?
Gramma! Coffee!
Me and Jason were gonna go get something to eat, too.
We were?

Oof!
Could you show us the way?
Oh my, yes.

Look at this boy, he is all skin and bone. Let's go.
Back in a bit!
I brought some things from home, better than this horrible food. I have plenty for everyone!

I really am glad you're okay.
And I'm so, so sorry about—

No. No sorrys. That wasn't your fault.
I made a choice. And I'd make it again.

Maybe leave the heroics to me next time, though?
Good. How're you feeling? For real?
Deal.
I'm okay. Sore. But I got a cool scar out of it.

Cool scar? Really?
Oh yeah. Girls dig scars. At least, I'm hoping one in particular does.

Sign of my bravery and all. She's a tough one, so I gotta look tough too.
Ha! Well, tell this girl you look fine just the way you are.

Even my funny face?
*Especially* your funny face.

What about you? Now that your secret's out...
I'm... I'm okay with it, I think.
For real?
For real. The video inspired people to come forward. Everyone's talking about what Wayland's done, and he won't be a danger to anyone else.

Besides, if being a hero means protecting those you love...
I can do that.

Save the day, get the guy. D didn't tell me about this part.
D?

Long story.
Tell me someday?

Someday.

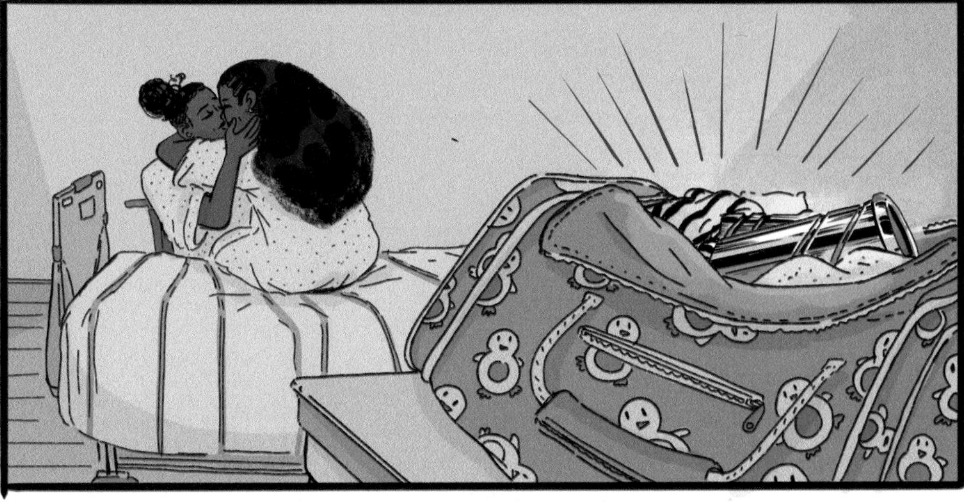

## RESOURCES

If you, or a loved one, need help in any way, you do not need to act alone. Below is a list of resources that may be helpful to you. If you are in immediate danger, please call emergency services in your area (9-1-1 in the U.S.) or go to your nearest hospital emergency room.

### The Jed Foundation

A nonprofit that exists to protect emotional health and prevent suicide for our nation's teens and young adults. Text "START" to 741-741 or call 1-800-273-TALK (8255)
Website: jedfoundation.org

### March for our Lives

Whether you are a survivor, activist, journalist, have lost a loved one to gun violence, or are experiencing secondary trauma, visit marchforourlives.com/mental-health-resources/ for more ways to seek proper support.

### Safe Horizon

The largest provider of comprehensive services for domestic violence survivors and victims of all crime and abuse including rape and sexual assault, human trafficking, stalking, youth homelessness, and violent crimes committed against a family member or within communities. If you need help, call their 24-hour hotline at 1-800-621-HOPE (4673) or visit safehorizon.org.

Photo by Nicole McLaughlin

Named one of The Root's and BET's 100 most influential African Americans of 2020, Leatrice "Elle" McKinney, writing as L.L. McKinney, is an advocate for equality and inclusion in publishing, and the creator of the hashtags #PublishingPaidMe and #WhatWoCWritersHear. A gamer and Blerd, her works include the Nightmare-Verse books, *Nubia: Real One* through DC, Marvel's *Black Widow: Bad Blood*, and more.

Robyn Smith is a Jamaican cartoonist, currently based in New York City. She has an MFA from the Center for Cartoon Studies and has worked on comics for the *Seven Days* newspaper, CollegeHumor, and the Nib. She's best known for her minicomic *The Saddest Angriest Black Girl in Town* and for illustrating Jamila Rowser's comic *Wash Day*. Besides comics, she spends most of her time watching American sitcoms and holding on to dreams of returning home, to the ocean.

Photo by Robyn Smith